D1442377

A Note to Parents and Caregivers:

Read-it! Readers are for children who are just starting on the amazing road to reading. These beautiful books support both the acquisition of reading skills and the love of books.

The PURPLE LEVEL presents basic topics and objects using high frequency words and simple language patterns.

The RED LEVEL presents familiar topics using common words and repeating sentence patterns.

The BLUE LEVEL presents new ideas using a larger vocabulary and varied sentence structure.

The YELLOW LEVEL presents more challenging ideas, a broad vocabulary, and wide variety in sentence structure.

The GREEN LEVEL presents more complex ideas, an extended vocabulary range, and expanded language structures.

The ORANGE LEVEL presents a wide range of ideas and concepts using challenging vocabulary and complex language structures.

When sharing a book with your child, read in short stretches, pausing often to talk about the pictures. Have your child turn the pages and point to the pictures and familiar words. And be sure to reread favorite stories or parts of stories.

There is no right or wrong way to share books with children. Find time to read with your child, and pass on the legacy of literacy.

Adria F. Klein, Ph.D.
Professor Emeritus
California State University
San Bernardino, California

Editor: Patricia Stockland
Page Production: Melissa Kes/JoAnne Nelson/Tracy Davies
Art Director: Keith Griffin
Managing Editor: Catherine Neitge
Page production: Picture Window Books
The illustrations in this book were rendered digitally.

Picture Window Books
5115 Excelsior Boulevard
Suite 232
Minneapolis, MN 55416
877-845-8392
www.picturewindowbooks.com

Printed in the United States of America.

Library of Congress Cataloging-in-Publication Data
Jones, Christianne C.
Chicken Little / by Christianne C. Jones ; illustrated by Kyle Hermanson.
p. cm. — (Read-it! readers: folk tales)
Summary: When an acorn hits her on the head, Chicken Little believes the sky is
falling down and runs to tell the King and everyone she meets along the way.
ISBN 1-4048-0972-4 (hardcover)
[1. Folklore.] I. Hermanson, Kyle, ill. II. Title. III. Series: Read-it! readers folk tales.

PZ8.1.J646Ch 2004
398.24'529353—dc22   2004018427

Chicken Little

By Christianne C. Jones
Illustrated by Kyle Hermanson

Special thanks to our advisers for their expertise:

Adria F. Klein, Ph.D.
Professor Emeritus, California State University
San Bernardino, California

Susan Kesselring, M.A.
Literacy Educator
Rosemount-Apple Valley-Eagan (Minnesota) School District

PICTURE WINDOW BOOKS
Minneapolis, Minnesota

One day, an acorn cracked
Chicken Little on the head.

"Oh my!" she cried. "The sky is falling! I must go tell the king."

Along the way, Chicken Little met Henny Penny. "Where are you going in such a hurry?" asked Henny Penny.

"The sky is falling!" cried Chicken Little. "We must go tell the king! Follow me!"

Soon, they met Cocky Locky. "Where are you two going in such a hurry?" asked Cocky Locky.

"The sky is falling!" yelled Chicken Little. "We must go tell the king! Follow us!"

Soon, they met Ducky Lucky. "Where are you all going in such a hurry?" asked Ducky Lucky.

"The sky is falling! We must go tell the king!" yelled Chicken Little. "Follow us!"

Soon, they met Goosey Loosey. "Where are you all going in such a hurry?" asked Goosey Loosey.

"The sky is falling! We must go tell the king!" cried Chicken Little. "Follow us!"

Soon, they met Turkey Lurkey. "Where are you all going in such a hurry?" asked Turkey Lurkey.

"The sky is falling! We must go tell the king!" yelled Chicken Little. "Follow us!"

So, Chicken Little, Henny Penny, Cocky Locky, Ducky Lucky, Goosey Loosey, and Turkey Lurkey hurried off to tell the king the sky was falling.

17

They were well into their trip
when they met Foxy Loxy.

"Where are you all going in such a hurry?" snarled Foxy Loxy.

They all cried, "The sky is falling! We must go tell the king!"

Chicken Little, Henny Penny, Cocky Locky,
Ducky Lucky, Goosey Loosey, and
Turkey Lurkey were so glad
Foxy Loxy was helping them
that they followed him
deep into the forest.

In fact, they followed Foxy Loxy right into his cave!

Chicken Little, Henny Penny, Cocky Locky, Ducky Lucky, Goosey Loosey, and Turkey Lurkey have been missing since that day.

And the king never did hear
that the sky was falling.

More *Read-it!* Readers

Bright pictures and fun stories help you practice your reading skills. Look for more books at your level.

FOLK TALES

Chicken Little by Christianne C. Jones

The Gingerbread Man by Eric Blair

How Many Spots Does a Leopard Have?
   by Christianne C. Jones

The Little Red Hen by Christianne C. Jones

How the Camel Got Its Hump by Christianne C. Jones

The Pied Piper by Eric Blair

Stone Soup by Christianne C. Jones

Looking for a specific title or level? A complete list of *Read-it!* Readers is available on our Web site: *www.picturewindowbooks.com*